Libertad

Alma Fullerton

Fitzhenry & Whiteside

Published in Canada by Fitzhenry & Whiteside,
195 Allstate Parkway, Markham, Ontario L3R 4T8

Published in the United States by Fitzhenry & Whiteside,
311 Washington Street, Brighton, Massachusetts 02135

www.fitzhenry.ca   godwit@fitzhenry.ca

10 9 8 7 6 5 4 3 2 1

Library and Archives Canada Cataloguing in Publication

Fullerton, Alma
       Libertad / Alma Fullerton.
ISBN 978-1-55455-106-4
   I. Title.
PS8611.U45L52 2008   jC813'.6   C2008-902323-4

**U.S. Publisher Cataloging-in-Publication Data
(Library of Congress Standards)**

Fullerton, Alma.
    Libertad / Alma Fullerton.
[224] p. : cm.
Summary: After their mother dies tragically, Libertad and his little
brother Julio live by their wits and what little they can earn as marimba
musicians in Guatemala City. Soon the two will head out on the long
and dangerous journey to the Rio Grande River, where they plan to
cross the border to America and find their father.
ISBN: 978-1-55455-106-4
1. Brothers—Guatemala—Juvenile fiction. 2. Guatemala—Juvenile
fiction. I. Title.
[Fic] dc22   PZ7.F8554Li   2008

Fitzhenry & Whiteside acknowledges with thanks the Canada Council
for the Arts, and the Ontario Arts Council for their support of our
publishing program. We acknowledge the financial support of the
Government of Canada through the Book Publishing Industry
Development Program (BPIDP) for our publishing activities.

Canada Council   Conseil des Arts
for the Arts   du Canada

ONTARIO ARTS COUNCIL
CONSEIL DES ARTS DE L'ONTARIO

Mixed Sources
Product group from well-managed
forests, and recycled wood or fiber
FSC   www.fsc.org Cert no. SW-COC-002358
© 1996 Forest Stewardship Council

Cover image by Pascal Milelli
Design by Kong

Printed in Canada

Libertad

To all of the children who have
successfully made their own journey;
to those children who have
come so far only to be turned back;
and especially to those children who
have died along the way.

Libertad

PART ONE

Dump Dwellers

Caught in a maze of high, white walls
that keep others from seeing them
salvage through garbage
and live like rats.

Los Niños Del Basurero

Atrapados en un laberinto de paredes blancas
para que otros no vean
que buscan desechos en la basura
y viven como ratas.

Marbles

Today is a good day, bringing
little surprises out of the trash,
their hints of sparkles calling
for me to rescue them.

And I do.

I kneel next to them, pulling
them from garbage graves, rubbing
crusted dirt off their glass
until they gleam, hiding
them safe in my pocket,
freeing
them from the garbage
                    forever.

Games

We make a small sanctuary,
Antonio, Esvin, and I,
where we can escape
for a short while
before dark.

My little brother Julio perches
on the edge of our broken couch, watching
us play.

When I win the shot,
I dance and sing an old song
of Papi's, stirring
faded memories from
a long time ago.

Julio laughs and sings with me.
He bounces on the couch,
its music mixes with mine,
so I jump up too,
coils beneath us, squealing
a Quetzal's song.
I take his hands in mine

and pretend we're flying
like birds.
Beautiful and free.

"Libertad," Antonio tells me,
"you act like street clowns."

"We aren't just street clowns," I shout.
"We're Clown Kings!"
I flip Julio and catch him, imagining
we're performing with Papi
on a street in America.
                    en América

But when the sun
slips behind the mountains,
I'm brought back here.

We collect our marbles, rushing
for the safety of our homes.
Tonight, even the moon is
afraid
to show its face
on our dump.

Home

I shiver and pull Julio closer,
making certain
the thin blankets on our single mattress
cover him too.

A breeze flaps the tattered curtain
that separates our shack into two rooms
and I see flashes of the other side:
a worn photograph of Papi
taped on the pressboard wall;
the wrinkles of Mami's face lit
by the glow of the lantern;
her eyes – glossy and semi-focused;
her elbow resting on the dirty table beside
an opened bottle of cobbler's glue;

her hand gripping a wrinkled piece of paper –

Papi's address.

Her long, calloused fingers wrap
around it like the dying branch of a tree
clings to its last leaf.

"One day, Libertad," she whispers,
Un día
"he'll come back for us
and we'll be
free."

My Freedom

Mi Libertad

Mi Libertad.
All I can think of.
It fills up my restless nights,
tastes sweet in my mouth.

Mi Libertad.
Over the mountains
and far beyond the borders
of a displaced life.

Mi Libertad.
Away from the dump.
North to where my papi
                    mi papi
                            lives
– the United States.

When I Was Seven

Five years ago, one cold evening came to our
    mountain village,
bringing with it brightly woven blankets and *mi papi*
home from the coffee fields
with his cousin's address scrawled on a piece of paper.

Five years ago, one cold evening, Papi told us he
    was leaving
to work in America, and the chill from outside
seeped through our wooden walls
and wriggled under my blanket, prickling
my body with its icy fingers.

Five years ago, one cold morning left our
    mountain village,
taking with it *mi papi*,
with dreams of someday returning
to us.

Five years ago, one colder morning came to our
    mountain village,
bringing with it soldiers
hidden behind masked faces,
rattling rifles slung over their shoulders,
and we left for here,
Guatemala City,
with hopes that someday Papi wouldn't return
to THEM.

Dreaming

Early morning light
creeps
into our ravine.

It caresses Julio's cheek
like a mother's gentle touch,
and he smiles.

I wonder if a lost memory is sneaking
into his dreams.
A memory of Papi
and music from his marimba.
Or the fresh smells of coffee fields
and clean air in the mountains.
But I know these memories sneak into
my dreams.

Not Julio's.

Julio only remembers
the dump.

But then sometimes I think
not knowing what
                    could be
is better,
because he doesn't
long for everything he's
missing.

Julio

I brush his hair from his face,
and sing, "Julio, Julio,

       wake up,
       my Julio,"
       despiértate,
       mi Julio

and tickle him awake.

He jumps and races through the door, laughing –
always laughing, *mi Julio.*
I chase him and put on his hat.
Today the sun won't beat down
on his head while
he works
and make him sick.

When Death Knocks

The sky is black with vultures
circling and diving for the burger
I found for our breakfast.

They hover over Julio
like Death,
knocking at his door
and waiting for him to answer.

I beat them back with a stick
and throw my food away from him.
Vultures swarm for it,
leaving Julio to eat in peace.
But instead of eating,
he breaks his half in two
and gives me one,
so Death doesn't knock
at my door.

I love him,
my brother
Julio.

Yo lo adoro,
mi hermano
Julio.

School

Esvin and his brother Mica pass us
as we work to collect sellable garbage
with thousands of others.
Esvin's and Mica's book bags bounce
off their legs as they race
for school.

Antonio laughs. "Look at them run, Libertad.
That school is for babies. You and I, we work
like real men."

He kicks at the dirt as he turns
to climb a mound of garbage.
When he thinks I'm not looking,
he stares back at Esvin and sighs.

I know we're both longing
to run to school with them, swinging
our book bags from side to side,
like I used to in my old village.

But today the only thing we're swinging
is our metal bars, poking
through heaps of garbage, looking
for cardboard to sell.

No strangers from America are sending
money for us.
And with our papis gone,
we have to be
here.

Julio is only seven,
but he's smart enough to go
to school.
He already knows how to
separate the garbage
into different piles.

Asking Mami

I ask Mami about sending
Julio to school.
She says, "We need him working
so we can have enough money to eat.
He can't go.
When Papi comes back for us,
Julio will go to school in America."

But Papi is taking too long,
and it'll be too late
for Julio.
Maybe, if I can save
enough money,
I can show Mami that
Julio can go to school now.

Music

Julio yanks at something.
The last of the garbage
clutching it gives way.
He tumbles
          backward,
crashing, plinking, clanging
down a hill of trash
toward me.

"Look," he says, wide-eyed,
arms stretched out, carrying
his prize.
"Can you play it, Libertad?"

A marimba.

I don't know
how it got into our pile
or how it came to find us,
but I'm grateful,
and with shaking hands
I take it.

Some of the keys are cracked,
but I know
I can make it come to life.

I pull away mallets attached to the sides
and tap out a tune Papi taught me
long ago . . .
hace mucho tiempo

Julio jumps and skips
around me, making
his own kind of dance.

Mami takes his hands
and dances with him,
humming, spinning, swaying
to my music.

For a while,
I dream we're back
in our village
and Papi is here.

But then our reality crashes
with sounds from a rumbling plow.
It pushes our memories into the gorge
with the noise of falling garbage,
and we know we must get back
to work.

Thief

When I turn to put the marimba beside my pile,
I see someone has stolen my cardboard.

Making Up Lost Time

The high sun scorches my back,
and my mouth is dry.
There will be no more playing
today.
I have to keep working
to make up for the cardboard
I lost.

Sorting
and working,
sorting
and working,
or there won't be enough to trade
for even two quetzals to add to Mami's money,
and I'll never show Mami I can
save
so Julio can go to school.

Gangs

The dying sun
drops in the sky,
and there are few workers left around me.
I should be back in my shack
with Mami and Julio,
so I gather my cardboard.

Gangs of men, teens, and children
lurk around the dump,
ready to jump on us
like vultures,
just because they can.

I avoid them, weaving
through piles of garbage, taking
the long way home.

Antonio's dog growls inside his cardboard house
as I step past it.
Antonio pokes his head between the blankets
thrown over the opening.
He turns and pats his dog's head.

"It's just Libertad, girl," he says to her.
"It's okay. He's no danger to us,
except maybe to our ears
when he tells us bad jokes."

I laugh as I continue home.
Sometimes, I worry about that funny Antonio,
all alone and living in a big box inside the dump.

I'm glad to have a tin-roof shack just outside of
   the dump.
We're safer from the gangs,
but we have more harassment from the police.
They don't step inside the dump walls.
If they did, they wouldn't protect us
because to them we are the
enemies,
enemigo
and their job is to
protect society
from us.

Safe

I curl up on our mattress with Julio and Mami.
Julio stirs and I pull him close.
"Don't be afraid," I whisper.
"I'm home now.
I'll protect you."

Puppies

Antonio's dog had puppies
– five of them –
and one is for me and Julio.

I want the biggest one,
but Julio chooses the runt.
He says the big one will soon
take care of himself,
but the runt will die without us.

Antonio and Esvin think
I'm crazy to agree with Julio
and take the runt.
But Julio is right.

With one hand,
I hold our puppy up high in the air.
"This is Guerrero!" I shout. "Warrior!"

Antonio and Esvin laugh
as my warrior yelps and pees down my arm
because he's scared to be so high in the air.

Long Days

Every day,
I work extra long
and try to hold back
a little of my money
for Julio to go to school,
like Papi would want me to.

Morning Marimba Lessons

The morning comes
with the sound of my marimba
as Julio bangs the keys.

I pull him onto my lap
and teach him to play a song
the way Papi taught me – moving
his hands with mine
and hitting the keys.

When he reaches for the right key
before I do,
my insides fill
with warmth from the rising sun.

I dig through my pocket
and hand him a marble.
"A reward for being Julio," I say.
Una recompensa

Julio grins and runs through the door
with Guerrero scampering close behind.
"I'm coming," he calls.

"We can start work now!"
He races for our neighbors' homes
like the foreman of our job site.

I smile at him,
my little brother Julio.
So small,
he doesn't know about the hate
that hovers over us like
a black cloud
of death.

I smile at Julio.
So small,
he still believes
everyone loves him.

I smile at Julio,
and I don't tell him
anything
different.
Because I love
my little brother
Julio.

Beans and Rice

We worked hard today, collecting
enough cardboard to sell so
we can have beans with our rice
and I can still keep a quetzal hidden
deep in my pocket with the others,
for Julio to go to school.

When we've eaten,
Julio tries to play his new piece for Mami,
but Guerrero keeps attacking the mallets.
We laugh and I pull the puppy away.
"No, Guerrero.
You can't eat those."

Julio taps out his tune,
and I make our puppy dance to the music.
When I look at Mami,
she's crying.
"Stop, Julio," I say.

He reaches to wipe tears off her face.
"I won't play, Mami," he says. "I won't make
you cry anymore."

Mami wraps him tight in her arms
and holds him close.
"No, Julio," she says. "You play.
I'm crying because I'm happy."
                    Estoy feliz

Julio grins
and continues
with his music.

Someday,
he will become a great marimba player
like Papi,
and that fills my heart
more than my stomach tonight.

Papi's Marimba

I close my eyes, imagining
Papi
somewhere in America, playing
his marimba under the starry sky, thinking
about coming to find us.

I close my eyes, imagining
Papi
somewhere in America, playing
his marimba for us.

And I wish,
more than anything,
I could hear it.

Underground Explosions

As we sleep,
the ground shakes with an explosion
somewhere in the dump.

I hope it's nowhere near Antonio
or one of the other workers
who live inside the dump walls.

I pull Julio closer, thanking
God
he's still safe
with me.

Being Tough

Julio cries out
when the vultures
steal his breakfast.

I pick him up,
wipe new dirt off his old dirt,
and tell him, "Courage, Julio, courage."
> *Valor, Julio, valor*
"If they see you cry,
they'll know they can take
anything from you."

"I'll be strong."
He stomps his feet
and gives me his meanest look.
"Like Libertad," he grunts.
Como Libertad

I kneel and look in his eyes.
"You are very strong, Julio."

He picks up a stick
to beat away
his own vultures.

I pray more that vultures
will see Julio is tough enough
and won't try to steal
from him.

Rain

The darkened sky carries a downpour, hitting
my shoulders and back, making them
heavy with water. Shivers numb
my body until I'm too tired to work.

But the jingle of Julio's money,
deep in my pocket,
mixes with the rain's tapping
on the garbage mounds.

Ching, ching, swish, swish.
Ching, ching, swish, swish.

And I have my own
dump-site orchestra, bringing
enough energy
to dance
while I work.

Good Marimba Players

Because of the rain,
we didn't make
enough money
to buy food for three.

Instead of giving Mami
some of Julio's school money,
I tell her
I'm not hungry.

I play my marimba
to Julio and Mami
while they eat.

"Libertad!" Esvin yells from outside.
"Bring that marimba here
so we can hear too."
I look at Mami and she nods.

A crowd of friends gather outside
our little shack.
Even grumpy Mariano,

from two doors down,
is smiling his toothless grin
and tapping his feet
through little puddles
to my music.

I smile, knowing
music is in my blood.

Papi told me that
making people forget
their troubles is what a
good marimba player
is supposed do.

Money

My pockets are weighed down
with money for Julio,
so I put it all in a tin can
and dig a hole in the dirt
beneath my mattress
to hide it,
so no one knows I have money.

Boys and Dogs

Guerrero stays by Julio's side,
watching over him
and us.

A guardian angel.

He barks when someone comes
close to our piles
or to Julio.

Julio saved Guerrero's life.
He knows,
and now he's rewarding Julio.

Fulfillment

Coins fill my tin can, glittering
as moon rays touch their shiny heads, bringing
closer dreams of Julio attending
school,
and with that, the knowledge
mi papi would be proud.

Safe Passage for Julio

Esvin takes me to the place called Safe Passage that
he says will get Julio
into school.

He brings me to a large room
with murals painted on the wall
and points to a woman
who is helping a boy read.
"Go see her," he says.

The woman turns from the boy
and looks a moment at my coins
clamoring against the table top
before looking at me,
confused.

"Is this enough money for school?" I ask.

"It's more than enough," she says gently,
lighting the room with a smile.
The knots in my stomach settle,
and I know Julio will be
treated with kindness here.

She gives me some school supplies.
"Go to the school every morning
and come here in the afternoon. We'll give you
a hot meal
every day,
and if you attend school regularly,
at the end of the month we'll give you a bag of
food to take home."

I follow her into another room,
this one filled with tables and benches.
She hands me a large bag of food,
more food
than what I would have bought
with the money I gave her.
"Take this home today. You've paid enough for it."

On top of the bag is a school uniform
too big for Julio
– a uniform for me.

"No," I say.
"I need a uniform for my little brother Julio.
He's seven."

Her expression shows something
I don't understand.
But then she smiles again
and gives me a smaller uniform too.
"It's enough for both of you."

I shake my head slowly.
"If I go to school,
Julio can't.
I have to work with Mami.
Julio will go.
I've been to school.
I can already read a little.
I want Julio to go."

Even though it's hard,
I hand her the big uniform
back.

Never Enough Money

Mami is shaking,
grasped in the arms of anger because
I spent money on school supplies for Julio when
we don't have enough money
to eat.

I give her the bag of food the teacher gave me.
I tell her Julio needs to go.
I tell her Julio is smart enough to go.
I tell her Papi would want Julio to go.
I tell her I'll work extra hard
so Julio can go.
And finally, after my pleading,
after my begging,
Mami's eyes go soft
and she says
yes.

And my head feels lighter
than Antonio's after he's had
a hit of cobbler's glue.

Christmas

This morning, Julio dances, hugging
his uniform in his skinny arms.
"I'm going to school?" he asks, unsure if I'm
joking with him.
"Really?"

"Yes, Julio," I say.
"In a few days, you'll go
to school, and you'll eat every day."

This morning Julio
dances.

Watching him,
I cry because that is the
greatest
gift of all.

I am happy.
Estoy feliz

Party

We're invited to Safe Passage
for a Christmas party.

My marimba and Mami's singing
fill his classroom with music
as students open gifts from strangers in America.

Julio hugs a stuffed bear, almost as big as him.
He dances with it, swaying
back and forth,
back and forth
to the music.
Esvin flicks a flashlight,
on and off,
on and off,
lighting up my mother's face
                        like a ghost.

Proud

Julio hasn't taken off his
school uniform
since Christmas morning.
I tell him it's going to get dirty
while we work today, so he strips it off
and climbs into his work clothes.
"Tomorrow I will go to school,"
he announces as he gently places
his folded uniform on his
dirty blankets.

He smiles at me.
"Tomorrow I'll make you proud."

I hug him hard, not wanting to
let go.
"I'm already proud, Julio.
You will always make me proud."

Bad Day

This is a good garbage day of cardboard and plastic bags.
Julio and Mami search rubbish heaps. As I stand guard,
The sun beats hot upon our backs through shirts of
    tattered rags.

Julio, small and spindly, trips on cardboard that he drags.
He rises tall with an unfazed grin. We're working so hard,
This is a good garbage day of cardboard and plastic bags.

Mami pokes a different heap but Julio still lags.
As he slurps on a melon rind and black vultures bombard,
The sun beats hot upon our backs through shirts of
    tattered rags.

Guerrero barks beside some kids as Julio plays tag.
I close my eyes and dream we stand in a schoolyard.
This is a good garbage day of cardboard and plastic bags.

Through the duration of the day my tired spirit sags.
Digging through richer men's trash with hands blistered
    and scarred,
The sun beats hot upon our backs through shirts of
    tattered rags.

A noisy dozer plows through with garbage-heaped zigzags,
Mami, unaware, though Guerrero's barking hard,
This was a good garbage day of cardboard and plastic bags.
Now the sun no longer beats upon her tattered rags.

Buried

Guerrero is barking
at a huge pile of garbage.
Guerrero is digging
at a huge pile of garbage.
Guerrero is digging
where my mother stood
just seconds ago.

No

"NO! Mami. NO!"

Julio and I tear through mounds to find
Mami.

We claw
and rip
and search through garbage.

Other workers dig with us,
frantically
dig with us, through mounds and mounds.
We dig to find my mother who is

   buried alive
beneath a pile of
    reeking,
     rotting
    garbage.

But soon the others
give up.

They've seen it before.
They give up
and go back to work,
relieved it's not their family,
relieved it's not them.

But I wish it were
their family.
I wish it were
them.
I wish it were
anyone
but
Mami.

Orphans

Julio and I dig
through the rest of the day.
We scour with only moonlight
protecting us from night
lurkers.
We search for Mami
so loving.

Mami
so beautiful.

We search
through piles of decaying
human waste
for Mami.

But we
Can't
Find
Her.

No
Podemos
Encontrarla

Please Dance

Julio sits beside the pile, wrapping
his arms around his knees and rocking
back and forth,
back and forth.

Guerrero lies beside him, whining.

I kneel beside them
with my marimba and play.

Music will bring Mami back.
She'll hear music and find her way out.
Mami loves us.
She loves the marimba.
She loves to dance.
She'll dance all the way back to us.

Mami will
come.

So I play
as loud as I can.

For hours, I play.
Even when my arms are sore
from banging on my marimba,
I play.

But this time when I play,
there's no dancing.
There's no laughter.
There are just silent stares
from my neighbors.

Still, I play
because Mami will come home.
They'll see.
Mami has to come home.
They'll see.
Mami WILL come home
when she hears my marimba.

So still
I keep playing
for Mami.

I keep playing
until I accept
what everyone else knows.
No matter how long I play,
Mami will
NEVER
come
home.

Julio sits beside the pile, wrapping
his arms around his knees and rocking
back and forth,
back and forth.

Heavy

My chest is weighed down
by the thought of the garbage and rocks
the bulldozer kicked up
when it buried Mami.
It hurts to breathe.

So sometimes
I don't,
but then my mind forgets
and I take a deep breath,
and it hurts
all over again,
and I wonder if it'll ever stop
hurting.

Dragging Him from Mami

Julio is sprawled on the mound of garbage
where Mami is buried,
and he kicks and screams as I pull him off
before the bulldozer
plows him and the garbage pile
into the gorge.

Garbage crashes down,
and my heart jumps with life
when I think I see the hand
that just days before
held Papi's address.
But when I look again,
it's gone.

And inside
I'm dead.
Estoy muerto

A Refuge

It's dark.
I doze on our mattress, dreaming
of a place where trees are green and I'm smelling
wildflowers instead of decay.

I doze on our mattress, dreaming
of a safe place without gas exploding
near our homes, or bulldozers plowing
over them.

I doze on our mattress, dreaming
of a place without groans from our bellies,
without the fumes of cobbler's glue
filtering through the air.

I doze on our mattress, dreaming
of a place just for us.

When Julio cries out in his sleep,
I know we have to find
that place.

Packing

Even though Julio won't go to school here anymore,
I want him to have his supplies
for when he does,
so I tuck Papi's address
safely inside
one of Julio's schoolbooks
and pack them, along with
my marimba and his uniform,
into his schoolbag.

I grab Julio's hand
and we run, bag swinging
side to side
as we leave
the dump.

Stolen Innocence

The streets are crowded.
Strangers cast us judging
glares as we weave around them,
looking for a safe place to stay.

To them we're
nothing
but lowly thieves.

Because we have no money
and no food,
I leave Julio and Guerrero sitting
on a park bench
and become a thief.

Caught

I'm not a good thief
and get chased
by the vendor whose apples
I stole.

But before he catches me,
I take a bite,
and the sweet taste stays
in my mouth
through his beating.

Police

We sleep too late,
and a policeman's stick
is hard on my back.
I press against the bench
in the early morning mist,
trying to escape my pain outside
and my hurt inside.

Before the policeman can hit him too,
I grab Julio
and I run,
    Yo corro
even when my heart aches.
I run,
even when I can no longer feel my legs.
I run,
even when I can no longer breathe.
I run,
until I can no longer feel pain.

The Woman

In an alley,
a woman's voice is calling,
"Julio."

"Mami," Julio cries,
racing toward the alley
arms open, ready to hug our mother.

"Julio, no."
I run after him.

He freezes ahead of me, seeing
not Mami but another mother hugging
her son. Hanging his head and crying,
he trudges back to me, hugging
only himself.

Wanting Home

We curl up inside an empty box
by the market,
Julio, Guerrero, and me.

Suddenly, I'm pulled from the box by my foot.
"Get out!" a teenaged boy screams.
Salga!
He drops the shoe-shine box he was carrying
and punches me.
Guerrero jumps, teeth bared, growling,
and the boy kicks him.
"Stupid puppy."
He spins on his heels and yells at me,
"This is my box. Find your own."

I want to yell at him
that we had our own box.
I want to yell that we had
a father and a mother.
I want to yell
and kick
and scream,
but instead

I pick up Julio and I run.

Yo corro

I run,
even when my heart aches.
I run,
even when I can no longer feel my legs.
I run,
even when I can no longer breathe.
I run,
until I realize
I have nowhere
to run.

Too Far

I put Julio down and collapse against a building.
Panting, Guerrero scampers up beside us
and lays his head on my lap.

I beg a man passing
for some food,
but he doesn't see us.
    él no nos ve

He doesn't want
to see us.

He has his own family to feed.
There is nothing left
for us.

Finally someone does see us
and spits on us.
"Go home," he says.

Except we have only a memory
of a home.
And *mi papi*,
too far away.
We can't get to him.
We can't do it
Alone.

It's so far.
Está tan lejos

Signs

My memories won't protect us
from the bigger children looking
for a place to sleep.
I slide under a stoop
only big enough for Julio, Guerrero,
and me.

Something crinkles beneath my knee,
so I pull it out.

A ten-quetzal note.

TEN quetzals.
Enough for some food.
Maybe enough for a shoe-shine box.

I turn the bill over in my hand,
so I see the face side and the bird,
the Quetzal,
flying high near the top.

A Quetzal.
A sign of luck.
A sign of
our freedom.
Nuestra libertad

And I know,
instead of food
or a shoe-shine box,
I'll use this money
for a trip on a chicken bus heading north,
toward America,
toward our freedom,
toward Papi.

And I grab Julio,
and we run.
    nosotros corremos

PART TWO

Freedom's Journey

Nothing good in life comes
without obstacles,
but it's your choice
to overcome those obstacles
or not.

Viaje Hacia La Libertad

En la vida,
nada bueno llega sin obstaculos,
pero podemos elegir si los vencemos
o no.

Chicken Buses

Camionetas

On the edge of the city, dawn rises
with multicolored school buses.
They fill with people,
animals, and chickens.

Julio and I sit watching
buses pass until one named *A Little More*
                              Un Poco Más
pulls up, and the driver yells,
"Antigua!"

Good-Bye, Guatemala City

Outside our window
the city fades,
a blur of gray in the early mist,
with its buildings shrinking
into memories,
lost in a world of
responsibilities, burdening
my heart with despair until we approach
a sea of green mountainsides, bringing
with them a new life full of
hope.

Playing Sardines

I'm crammed between an old woman
and an English couple. Guerrero sleeps
beneath us, and Julio's on my lap, leafing
through his schoolbook.

I point to the alphabet
and read the letters out loud for him.
He repeats them.

Our lesson is interrupted
when another man attempts to slide onto
a slice of our seat, where he can't find a sliver,
so is left sitting on air.

When the bus swerves around
another curve in the road,
we slide even closer to the English woman,
and she frowns.

"I'm very sorry, *señorita*," I say.
Lo siento muchísimo

She smiles and turns to her companion.
"How many more people are they letting
on this bus?"

I smile, remembering the bus's name.
"A little more," I whisper to Julio.
Un poco más

Missing Mami

The bus squeals and stops with a jerk.
"Let the passengers off first," the driver calls.
He jumps off the bus and leans over
to jam a block of wood under the tire
so we won't roll backward
down the hill.

The old woman beside us
and the man sitting on air push their way
between other passengers
and toward the door.
Vendors call through the open windows,
selling their food and drinks to anyone
with money.

A Mayan woman dressed in
bright colors boards with a small child slung
across her chest and three others, carrying
caged chickens, in tow.

Memories of Mami
stir in my mind
like a warm meal.
She dressed in the same
bright colors
when we lived in our village,
only changing into the dull, worn colors
of the dump after
Papi left
and we moved.

Julio leans forward,
stretching to peek over the seat
at the family.
They approach, their chickens squawking
as the children bang the cages
against their legs.

Julio reaches for the woman,
touching her woven skirt, hopeful as she brushes
past him. He jerks his hand away
with the bang of a chicken cage
against our seat.

A single feather floats through the air
like an angel, landing
on Julio's shoulder.
I pick it up, tucking
it deep in my pocket,
to remind me
Mami will always be
with us.

Antigua

Antigua comes with the afternoon sun
shining through the chicken-bus window.

I wake Julio, lifting
his head off the English woman's shoulder
before the bus jerks to a stop
and she wakes too.

He scratches at his head, leaving
me wondering if he's shared
his lice with her, even though earlier
she never attempted to share
her bags of food with us.

She scratches at her head
and I smile.

I think Julio was very
generous to share what he has,
even though he has
so little.

Chicken Tortillas and Beans

Good smells are filtering
through the air, teasing
my empty stomach, pulling
me toward the food stand, paying
the vendor the remaining five quetzals hiding
deep in my pocket, making
me wonder if giving
up a bus ride to the next town is worth eating
chicken tortillas and beans and washing
it down with Pepsi in a bag.

From the smile on Julio's face . . .

I imagine, yes.
Se me figura que si

Fresh Air

As we're cradled by the branches of a tree,
the sweet smell of flowers
wakes up my insides,
unclogging the stale air left there from
Guatemala City.

Julio whimpers and I pull him close,
whispering the same stories of America
Papi used to tell me on quiet nights
like this, until I feel his weight
against me and know
he's
sleeping.

Markets

With the rising sun,
the market comes alive
with vendors.

Julio and I gaze at the different stands
as people sell everything from live animals
to handmade trinkets.
We only stop when I think I see Maria,
an old woman from our old village,
selling pottery and painted masks.

I speak to her and find out she's not
Maria but someone named Sophia,
and she doesn't shoo us away,
thinking we're thieves,
like the other vendors do.

Instead, she shares her fruit with us
and listens to our stories
of Mami and Papi.

Julio jumps and pats at our bag,
saying, "Can I show her how
I can play the marimba?"
I pull it from my bag
and let him play his song.
Then I play with him,
bringing tourists to her stand.
Because of our music,
she has a good selling day.

Later, Sophia asks if we'll come back tomorrow,
but we tell her we have to move on.
She gives us money for playing
and wishes us luck on our journey.

With her money, and the money some of the tourists
dropped in our bag as we played,
we have enough for some market fruit
and a chicken-bus ride
to Totonicapán.

Totonicapán

Our bus passes the bare fields cascading
over the hillsides of Totonicapán.
"It'll be a good year for planting,"
the man next to me says to no one in particular.
He turns to me.
"My name is Santos.
I help my sister's husband Enrique
farm near here."

I perk up, looking at the fields, knowing
in a month it'll be March – planting season –
and there will be work for me here too,
if we stay.

But my memories pull me
toward America.
If we move on to Mexico,
instead of waiting for planting season,
I can find some other kind of work there,
and we'd be that much closer
to Papi.

Hitching a Ride

We trudge alongside the highway
toward Quetzaltenango.
Julio jumps as a truck passes
and honks its horn.

It pulls over ahead of us,
and Santos opens the door, calling,
"Do you need a ride?
We can take you as far as the farm,
almost to Quetzaltenango."

We jump into the back of the truck.
Santos opens the window of the cab.
"This is Enrique."

"Hello," I say. "Thanks for the ride."

Julio and I hold tight
as Enrique bumps the truck
back onto the highway.

A horn blares again
as the truck barely avoids a chicken bus
passing on the wrong side of the road.
The bus veers into its own lane,
then tries to pass another car,
almost hitting a bigger truck
before squeezing into its own lane again.

Julio gasps and holds onto me.
"I don't know which is worse," I tell him,
"bumping in the back of this truck,
or having to be on that bus."

The bus veers into the other lane once more.

"Being on that bus." We laugh at the same time,
watching it disappear down the highway.

Dinner Guests

A woman and two girls
stand outside the door
of an adobe house
as we pull up
in front.

They wave excitedly to Santos
and run to kiss him on the cheek.
"Who do we have here?" the woman asks,
seeing us in the back of the truck.

"Stowaways." Enrique smiles.
He lifts Julio from the truck,
and Guerrero and I jump out after him.
"This is my wife Rosa.
These are our daughters
Genna and Marlita."

Rosa picks Julio up and tickles him.
"This one looks hungry." She laughs.
"Come eat. Dinner is ready." She carries Julio

into the house before I can tell her we
can't stay.
By the time I get inside,
Julio has a plate of food
in front of him.
I can't take it away,
so I say, "I guess we can stay,
but just for dinner."

Rosa tsks. "I will not have
two children leave my house
to walk to Quetzaltenango
in the dark. You must stay
for the night."

Genna laughs.
"When Mami has her mind set,
there's no changing it."

So I agree,
just for the night.

Morning

Before we leave,
Rosa gives us satchels of food,
two blankets, and bottles of water.
"You're sure you can't stay for planting season?"
she asks.

"We have to find my father."

"Good luck on your journey, then," she says.
She stoops to give Julio
a kiss on his cheek and hugs us
both good-bye.

Cold

In the mountains, I shiver.
The air is thinner up here,
and it's hard to catch my breath
as we walk toward Quetzaltenango.
"Are you warm enough?" I ask Julio, tucking
his blanket tighter around his shoulders
and fixing mine too.

"Yes," he says through chattering teeth.

"It'll be warmer soon," I say,
"when we get to Mexico.
Maybe there I'll find some work
to make money to get us to America faster."

Soon we can see the city lights sparkling
below us, and surrounding
us are treasures of coffee fields, making
me long even more for
mi papi, and I know
we've made the right choice
not to wait to move on.

Quetzaltenango

Julio weeps silently
as we huddle together
on a park bench.
I squeeze him tighter.
"It's okay, Julio. We'll be okay," I whisper.
"We're going to find Papi.
He'll take care of us."
He curls into my arms, wiping
his tears on my shirt, and I kiss his head.
"When we get to the United States, we'll find him.
Wait, Julio.
Wait and see.
Things will be good
there."

I look at the stars and pray
that I'm right.

Sunday

What luck. It's market day in Quetzaltenango.
Vendors from the neighboring
villages crowd the park.
Remembering how we made money in Antigua,
I make a deal with a man selling
brightly woven blankets
to play and bring people to his stand.

He tells us yes,
but at the end of the day
he doesn't pay us
anything.
"I would have sold as much
without you," he says.
"Now go away."

I don't argue and pull Julio behind me.
"That's not right," Julio says.
"We had a deal."

"There's nothing we can do, Julio.
If we argue,
he'll call the police.
Besides, the tourists have dropped enough quetzals
    in our bag
for a chicken-bus ride
to the Mexican border."

Border Crossing

Julio and I stop at the bridge,
watching as people cross to and from
Mexico.

Some reach the guards and are turned back.
I know they can turn us back too, or maybe arrest us,
or insist we pay them to go across.
We have no money to pay.
We must go on.

"Guerrero, come."
I take a deep breath
and grab Julio's hand.
Together we march across
the bridge.

The guard looks down at us
when we approach.
He stops us. "Where are you from?"

I swallow.
Courage, Libertad. Courage.
Valor

"Guatemala," I tell him.
"Where are you going?" he asks.

"The United States," I say.

He raises his eyebrows.
"Is that so?"

"Yes, *señor*.
To our papi," Julio says.

"Your father is in the United States?"

"Yes, *señor*," I tell him.

He bends and stares, inches
away from my face, giving me a hard look.
I think my knees are going to buckle
and he's going to send us back.

He straightens, smiles, and tousles my hair.
"Good luck, boys."
Buena suerte
"I hope you find your papi."

I let out the breath I was holding,
grab Julio's hand, and race across the border
before the guard changes his mind.
But he only yells after us, "Be careful!"

"Are we in Mexico?" Julio asks,
when I stop running.

"Yes, my brother."
    mi hermano
"We are in Mexico."

Work

A man follows close
behind us until he catches up.
"I overheard. You're going
to America?" he asks.

"Yes."

"Me too. My name is Fernando.
My wife and children
are in California," he says, pulling
a picture from his pocket – his wife
and two small children, perhaps the same age
as Julio.

"Why aren't you there too?" I ask.

"I was caught by Immigration and
deported back to Honduras."

"But you're going back?"

"Of course." He smiles.
"But first, I must go to Tapachula
to make money for my trip.
My cousin Carlos works in a factory there.
He's got a job for me."

"Do you think there'll be
a job
for me too?" I ask.

Julio looks up, "But —"
I glare at him and he shushes.

"There are a lot of jobs there," the man says
before he moves on.

I grab Julio and swing him.
"First to Tapachula,
where I'll find a job,
and then north
to the United States!"

Factory

Ovens glow, heat blasting
my face as I remove fat, golden cakes
from their warm bellies.
The cakes deflate,
hot air seeping out
as they move down the production line,
changing them into the tortillas I know.

While I Work

I worry about leaving Julio alone
while I work,
but there are other kids
on the streets,
and Guerrero is with Julio,
so he'll be safe.

Good Days

Every day,
I earn enough money
to buy food and a few clothes
and still keep some aside for our
journey.

Today, I make a little more,
so I'm able to buy Julio
a surprise.

After dinner, before taking
out my marimba to play,
I give it to him.

Julio smiles, showing
me his teeth and tongue turning
bright red from
the sweet surprise
melting inside
his mouth.

Direction

As I work, the man next to me says,
"To get through Mexico, go along the railway,
   not the highway.
Blend in with the Mexicans.
Make it look like you belong here
and always watch for coyotes."

I had heard about these men called coyotes
back in Guatemala.

My uncle Mario tried to pay one to transport him
to America in a coffee truck,
but the immigration patrols lining
the Mexican/US border were thick.

The coyote ran, leaving the truck
under the afternoon sun
with my uncle and thirty other people
trapped inside.

I miss my Uncle Mario.
He was a good man.

Moving On

Planting season has come to Mexico,
and I'll find work on a farm.
Working in the factory, I've saved
sixty pesos, and I know
it's time to
move on.

The Trains

We trudge alongside the tracks winding
through the countryside with trains whizzing
past us as we watch other immigrants hitching
illegal rides on the train tops, jumping
from car to car, seeing
soldiers waiting
ahead and sometimes catching
the immigrants, pulling
them from the trains, taking
them away, sending
them
home.

I don't
want
that.

Old Woman

The sun sets.
Outside a wooden shack
near Acapetagua,
an old woman stares down the tracks
at people walking by.

When a young, slim man nears,
she grins and races to embrace him,
crying, "Gabriel, Gabriel!"

He looks at her, startled,
and shakes his head.

Her smile falls and she lets go.
Discouraged, she stumbles back up the hill
   to her shack,
where she stands and stares down the tracks
at people walking by,
until she sees another young, slim man below.

Later, when we get to the train station,
I ask a carpenter, who is fixing a roof,
about the woman.

"Alicia," he says.
"Long ago, at the beginning of the war,
when her village was
overrun
by soldiers,
she left Guatemala with her son.

Along the way,
her son was taken away
by the soldiers.
She's still waiting for him
to come down the tracks
and find her."

"But if he was taken,
he'd be dead."

The carpenter looks into my eyes
and nods. "Yes, but still
she waits."

I Wonder

I hug Julio close
during the night
as we doze in a tree
near the station.

I wonder if Papi is sitting
somewhere in America, waiting
for us to come find him.
And when we do,
will he rush to hug us
the way Alicia hugged a man
who wasn't her son?

Lessons Learned

In the market,
in a village after Pijijiapan,
we buy some tortillas with beans
and sit on a bench to eat.

Before I can put my change away,
a man rushes up behind us,
pushes me to the ground,
and steals my money satchel.

Guerrero jumps at him
and the man rushes away,
leaving me lying on the ground
with my face
smooshed into my tortilla.
My spirit disappears
down an alley with Guerrero
as he chases the man.

"Will he get our money back?" Julio asks,
wide-eyed.

"I don't know," I say,
putting the few pesos I have left
deep into my pocket
and slouching on the bench,
my head in my hands.
How can I expect to get
to Papi
if I don't even know not to show
thieves where I keep my money?

Julio hands me my squished tortilla.
"Do you think Guerrero will come back?"

"We'll wait. He'll come."
A few minutes later,
he does.

He doesn't have my satchel,
but he does have a back-pocket chunk
of the man's pants
dangling in his mouth,
and that makes me feel
much better.

Shoes

Julio sits on a bench
and swings his feet so the cool air
flows through the holes
our journey
has made in the soles
of his shoes.

The Farmer

White hair pokes beneath a sombrero framing
his face, deep lines etch their way through it, marking
him with wisdom. His dark eyes winking
at us as we stand across the tracks, watching
him bellow with a deep laugh,
as the man beside him
tells him a joke.

His laugh is contagious,
and Julio and I
laugh too.

He smiles at us.
"My name is Manuel Barrio," he says.
"I need two farmhands to do some planting.
Do you boys know anyone willing to work?"

'We can do it," Julio offers
before I say anything.

"Is that so?" Manuel asks.
"You'll work hard?"

"Yes," Julio says.

"And your dog?
He won't dig up my seeds?"

"No, sir," I say.
"Guerrero is a good dog."

"All right, then.
Come with me."

Luisa

Smells of cornbread drift from the kitchen
where we find an old woman singing.
Her graying hair is twisted at the back of her head
in a bun, her dress sways with her as she
stirs something in a pot.

Her voice lifts my heart
from my chest
like Mami's used to,
and I sigh.

"Did you find some help?" she asks
before she turns to face us.
"Oh my." She looks at Manuel
and smiles.
"This is my wife Luisa," he says.
"Luisa, may I present
 Libertad and Julio?"

"They can help?" she asks.
"They're kind of small."

"*Si*," he says.
"They can help."

"Very well," she says,
"but first they must wash
and eat.
After a good night's sleep,
they can work."

Planting

Row after row
I plant yellow kernels,
and after a few months
they'll grow
into strong cornstalks
so thick they could hide
a whole dump site
of illegal immigrants.

Manuel's Laugh

Every morning we eat
breakfast at a table
with Manuel and his wife Luisa.
After, we go to the fields
and plant corn or beans.

Every day at noon,
before our siesta,
Luisa comes out with a tray
of food and cold drinks,
and we sit on the ground in a circle
and eat a picnic like a
real family.

Every day, Manuel's laughter
fills up a hole deep inside me
I thought no one
could find.

Me and Manuel

Bumping down the highway
in a truck,
toward the village market
to pick up a few things
for Luisa.

He buys a special treat
just for me.
We talk about things
men talk about
and laugh and joke around
like only a father
and son could.

Julio and Luisa

Julio helps Luisa with her
little garden.
He helps her in the house
and goes for walks with her.

She watches over him
and plays with him
and hugs him
like a real mother.

Proposition

Manuel walks across the field
to where I'm planting.
"Libertad," he says.
"You know we have no children
of our own. No one to look after
the farm when we're gone."

I nod and plant another seed.

He clears his throat.
"Luisa . . .
Luisa and I
would like very much
for you and Julio to stay
with us
forever."

My heart aches
because Manuel fills the hole
Papi left there,
so I want to say,

Yes,
I want to
stay.

But I think about Papi,
and how Mami would want us
to go with him,
and how we should be
with him.
I think about his marimba
filling up our nights.
I think about *mi libertad*
and Julio's.

Then I think about Julio
with Luisa,
and how he smiles and laughs
with her tender touch
as she wipes his face clean
and hugs him close.

I look at Manuel
and see Papi in him.
I see his eyes sparkle
and hear his laughter.

I want to stay,
but instead I say,
"We can't.
We have to find Papi."

"I understand."
Manuel's shoulders slump,
and there's no laughter
from him
filling me up
today.

And I know,
now that the planting is done,
it's time for us
to move on
again.

Rebellion

Julio doesn't want
to go.
He won't pack his things.
He says he's tired of not having
a home.
He says he's tired of always
moving.
Julio doesn't want
to go.
He screams he wants to stay
here with Manuel and Luisa.
He screams
he's happy
here.

Luisa says
he can stay.

Manuel says
I can come back
with my father
to get Julio, later.

And the more he puts up
a fight,
the more he makes me think
he'd be better off
here.

He'd be safer
here
than traveling with me
to America.

The more I think of it,
the more I think
it's right for Julio,
to leave him
here.

But my heart has already
lost so much
it can't bear
to lose Julio too.

So I shove his things into our pack,
grab his hand, and drag him to Manuel's truck.

"You're coming
with me."

Always Welcome

Back in town,
Manuel buys us
two bus tickets to Mexico City
and a new pair of shoes each,
then hands me 300 pesos.
"For the help," he says.
"Remember, you're always welcome
in my home."

And he hugs us both
good-bye.

Snubbed

Julio refuses
to look at me.
He refuses to
speak to me.

He just stares out the bus window,
refusing to acknowledge
I'm even alive,
and right now
I feel I might as well
be dead.

Searching for a Smile

The silence between us
rests heavy
on my shoulders,
a burden harder to bear
than leaving Julio behind.

"Are you hungry?" I ask.
"Luisa packed us some food."

Without looking at me,
Julio holds up his own bag of food.

"How about a little music, then?
Do you want to learn a new piece
on the marimba?"

He moves closer
to the window.

"How about some lessons, then?
You know, you're doing so well.
I bet you'll be reading
before we see Papi."

Julio yawns
and closes his eyes.

So I pull out one of his workbooks
and pretend to read a story out loud.
Except I change names
to people we knew
back in the dump,
and I make them do
silly things,
all while sneaking peeks
at Julio, who is trying hard
to pretend he's not smiling
in his sleep,
and that makes me
smile again too.

A Boy and His Dog

Guerrero lies
whimpering through the mesh cage
he was forced to travel in
for the bus ride.

The door creaks
as it springs open when we unlock it,
freeing our dog. He jumps at Julio playfully,
knocking him to the ground
and licking his face.

The sound of Julio's laughter
fills me up, knowing everything
will be okay.

Mexico City

Streams of traffic honking
angrily though miles and miles of buildings towering
unforgiving over streets crowded with people dodging
expertly in and out of shops or offices. We keep
   wandering,
unobserved by the adults around us, pausing
to watch the various street performers hustling
at every intersection until we stop stumbling,
exhausted, upon an enormous park and are left feeling
overwhelmed with our first introduction to
Mexico City.

Pedro

The buildings around the park
block out the setting sun,
making it darker.

As we settle on a park bench,
I'm startled by something
moving.

"Julio," I whisper.
"There's a boy watching us."

"Where is he?" Julio glances around.

"In the tree. Don't look at him."
I pull our bags closer to me
and pat Guerrero's head,
hoping the sight of the dog
might scare the boy off
if he plans to steal
from us.

"You don't want to sleep there,"
the boy calls down.
"If you do, you'll likely be beaten
and robbed by street gangs."

las maras

"Where should we go?"

"There's room in my plaza," he says,
"if you want to follow me."
He jumps from the tree.

The boy is only about my size,
and he can't possibly be as
dangerous as _las maras_,
so I shrug and gather our bags.

"I'm Pedro," the boy says
as we follow him through the park
and into a plaza.

Pedro's Plaza

Smells of solvents
snap under my nose.
My eyes adjust to darkness
creeping
over the plaza.

"This is my place," Pedro says.
"You can sleep with us."

Us?

I look around and see
several children
lay blankets along the walls
of surrounding monuments.
One of them sets up a black and white
television,
and another is washing his pants
in the fountain.

"Great home, isn't it?" Pedro says.
"Yes," I agree.

"I'm the King here,
so I won't let anyone
hassle you," he says
as he sprawls himself
in front of the television.
"Come sit.
It's a good show."

"Thank-you."

Julio glances at me as I lay our blankets
beside Pedro's.
I shrug and whisper,
"Better here with a lot of kids
than out there
alone."

Morning

Sunrays prod my eyes.
I try to squint them away,
but it's no use, so I yawn
and open them.

A boy next to me stretches
and looks at me. "You're new."

"Yes," I say.
"My name is Libertad.
This is Julio."

"I'm Marco." He smiles.
He shakes Pedro awake.
"I need a hit."

The Keeper

Pedro pulls a solvent-soaked tissue
from deep inside a plastic jar
and hands it to Marco.

Marco presses it to his face
and inhales deeply.

I glance around the plaza.
Pedro is the smallest child here.

I wonder what he did
to become the
Tissue Keeper.

The Sandwich Truck

Twice a week
there's a truck that comes, bringing
loads of sandwiches and drinks
just for us.

King Pedro

I listen to him command them
like he's King of the Plaza.

I watch as the others follow him
like he's a rock star.

I watch the girls bow down
at his feet
as he breaks up their
fights.

I watch as he charms
money from the passersby
without offering anything
back.

No music.
No dance.
No work.
Just charm.

I watch his actions,
the way he walks,
the way he talks,
his smile.

I watch him
and know why
he's the Tissue Keeper.

I watch him
and want to be just like
King Pedro.

Trying to Forget

Pedro pulls out
a soaked tissue
and takes a hit.

It reminds me of Mami
and Antonio,
and everyone else at the dump,
because they all sniffed glue.

It reminds me of the time I tried it
and didn't like it because it made me
forget bits of Papi.

When Pedro sees me
watching him,
he says, "It makes you
feel good and forget
about your troubles."

"What do you need
to forget?" I ask.

"I forget." He smiles.
"What do you need to forget?"

I think about the soldiers
and the dump
and Mami being buried alive
and how Papi is so far away
and how I have to look after Julio
alone.

I think about how our pesos
are dwindling because I have to buy food,
and how far we still have to go,
and how I just don't know
HOW
we'll get to Papi anymore.

So when Pedro hands me a tissue,
I take a hit.

High

I've spent the last of our pesos
on solvent.
The sandwich truck
only comes sometimes,
but I don't need to buy
food anyway.

The solvent makes me

FORGET

we need food.

Hustling

In English I know,
"I'm hungry."

In English I know,
"Can you spare some change?"

In English I know
how to hustle.

Tourists are suckers
for children who can speak
a little
English.

Prince Libertad

Pedro likes me.
He says I'm a natural hustler.

Pedro likes me
and has made me
a Prince.

Now I can hold
a tissue jar too.

Fading Dreams

Pedro asks me,
"Who taught you English?"

"My father," I answer.

"Where is he?"

"America."

"Are you going to America?"

"Yes."

"I'm going to be a doctor," Pedro says.

"You have to go to school to be a doctor," I tell him.

"Little by little," he answers.
Poco a poco
"You have to leave here
to get to America."

"Little by little," I answer in English.

But I'm tired
and we still have so far to go.
I was crazy
          loco
to think
we ever could make it in the first place,
and *poco a poco*
I wonder if we should
give up
and just stay here
in Pedro's Plaza.

Moving

Julio moves
his blanket
to the other side
of the plaza.

He says, "The smell
is too strong here
for Guerrero.
The solvent
makes him
act strange."

But I think
it's Julio
who is acting
strange, not the dog.

Solvent wouldn't
make a dog
strange.

Realization

There's a new kid
at the plaza.
Amando.

He sits beside me
as Pedro introduces us.
"Libertad is a good name
for a street kid," he says.

"I'm not a street kid."

"No?" His smile turns into a smirk.
"What are you, then?"

I'm too slapped
down
by his words
to answer.

Julio Asks

Julio washes in the fountain.
"Do you want to come
to the sandwich truck
to play the marimba
today?" he asks.

"Julio, it's silly to work
when you can just ask,"
I say.

"You sound like Pedro,"
Julio says as he grabs
my marimba.

"Thank you," I say,
pulling a tissue from my jar.

He looks at the ground
and mumbles,
"I wasn't saying it
to be nice."

All For a Sandwich

I'm hustling with Pedro
when Amando runs to us.

"The police," he says,
trying to catch his breath,
"are beating
the street children
gathered by the sandwich truck."
He stops to look at me.

"Julio is there."

Beaten

Sprawled in an alley
near the Alameda Central
of Mexico City
I find Julio,
beaten and bleeding.

I pick him up
and carry him
two blocks to the
program center for help.

I should have been
watching him,
but I wasn't.

It's my fault.

I am more
beaten
than Julio.

Enough

It's late in the evening when we get back
to the plaza.
Julio slowly packs his things
into our bag.

"Where are you going?" I ask him.

"What do you care?" he says.

"I care," I say.
"You're my brother."

"All you care about is this."
He picks up my plastic jar of tissues
and throws it hard against
the monument where we sleep.

It bounces off and rolls
into the center of the plaza,
where I scramble for it
before someone else picks it up.

Julio turns and looks me
straight in the eyes.

"You're no brother
of mine."

No

I grab Julio's arm.
Guerrero growls at
ME
like he doesn't know me.

"You can't leave me," I say.
"You're all I have left."

Julio pulls away.
"I'm going."

"Alone?"

"Better alone
than stay here with you."

Then *my little brother*
walks away
with Guerrero on his heels.

"I'm coming!" I yell to Julio.

He turns and nods.
"Good."

And for a moment
I wonder
which brother
is taking care
of which.

Leaving

Escaping the enormous park, stopping
at every intersection, playing
my marimba for the tourists who pause, dropping
change into my bag as they are dodging
expertly in and out of shops or offices. We leave,
    wandering
through streams of traffic honking
angrily though miles and miles of buildings, feeling
relieved as we head north, leaving
Mexico City.

On the Road

Cars whiz by us,
most drivers too busy
or too rushed
to notice two boys
walking
on the edge of the road.

We jump as a van
swerves in front of us
and some men get out.
"Immigration!"
they cry.

When we back away,
they grab us, and Guerrero,
and pull us into the van.

I struggle to get loose,

then see . . .
"Immigration officers
don't carry musical instruments."

The men laugh.
"No," one of them says.
"We saw you playing your marimba
in Mexico City
and thought you might need a lift."

"We musicians have to
stick together," says another.

"So, do you need a lift somewhere?"
the driver asks.

Julio and I look at each other.
"Yes!"

The Band

We share a name,
the band and I,

Freedom.
La Libertad

Elías, Ramón, Rafael, and Héctor.
They say we were
destined
to meet.

I think so too.

San Miguel de Allende

La Libertad plays for a wedding
in the town of
San Miguel de Allende.

Julio and I play too.

The women cackle
like hens
over my little brother.

They kiss his cheeks
and dance with him.

I haven't seen Julio
have so much fun
since we left Manuel's house.

Heaven

Water sprinkling
down over me, calming
all the nerves jumping
inside me that make me
want a hit.

I don't think
I'll ever leave this
hotel shower.

Early Morning Practice

When the sun wakes,
so do we.
After I go outside
to check on Guerrero,
we set up our instruments
and practice until it's time to pack up
and head to the next town
for the next wedding.

Ciudad Victoria

Julio is bouncing
on his heels beside me
as we enter the hotel
in the city of Ciudad Victoria,
where we are going to play.

Behind the glass,
inside a large room,
there is a real swimming pool
like the one we once saw
on Pedro's fuzzy television.

I turn to Rafael.
"Are we staying here?"

"Yes." He smiles.

"Here?" Julio asks again.

"Yes, Julio, here.
The father of the bride
is paying for us to stay here."

Food

The bride's father says,
"Help yourselves to the buffet, boys."

Julio's eyes grow wide
as we enter a room with
rows and rows
of food
covering clothed tables.

"There's enough food here
to feed everyone in the dump," I whisper.

"And Guerrero too," he says, stuffing
two extra buns and some roast beef
in his pocket.

Chocolate

Strawberries,
apples,
oranges,
pineapple,
bananas.
Even rubbery snails
taste good when dipped
in melted chocolate.

I will never be able
to eat garbage
again.

The Show

As I play my marimba,
I can hardly make my feet
stay still.

Julio dances beside me like he's got
fire ants racing up his legs.

When we finish our set,
Ramón puts down his banjo,
smiles, and whispers, "Go."
                    Vayan

POOL TIME!
WAHOOOO!
SPLASH!

Parting Ways

Héctor shakes me awake.
"It's time to go," he says.

I rub my eyes and roll
out of bed.
But I want to curl back up
and go back to sleep.
Today, I know
La Libertad is going
back to Mexico City.

Julio and I are going north,
and we'll have to say
good-bye to friends
again.

Ramón hands me 400 pesos.
"Your share," he says.
We help them load their instruments,
and they drive us to see
one of their friends,
who is bringing us to Monterrey.

"After Monterrey," Héctor says,
"be very careful of
immigration patrols and checkpoints.
They get thicker the closer
you are to the border."

I nod.

We hug good-bye.
And they watch
as we pull away
in their friend's van.

Monterrey at Night

A beam of red light
shines from a light tower
in the center of Monterrey.

The beam circles the city,
enclosing us all
safely inside.

Terror

A man follows us
along the road.

"I can get you
across the border," he says.
"I have a truck.
You can ride under the seats
for a price."

"No," I say.
"We aren't going that way."

He doesn't take
no for an answer.
"I'll get you across."

"We aren't going to the
United States,"
I lie.

"Where are you going, then?"

"Just to Nuevo Laredo."

"To visit our uncle,"
Julio says.

But the man says,
"I'll take you there, then.
Just give me
some money."

"No," I tell him.

He grabs Julio
and brings him close.
He holds a knife
close to his throat
and yells, "Give me your money,
or I'll kill him!"

I clench my teeth
as anger builds inside me
like the banging
on a drum.
I want to thrash the man

so hard he'll never get up,
but he has the knife
and I want to get Julio away
more than I want my money.
So I reach for it.

But before I can pull it out,
Julio's eyes go wide
as Guerrero jumps
at the man.

Guerrero clamps onto the man's arm
with his teeth.
The man jerks back,
screaming,
dropping the knife.

He falls
with Guerrero still
attached to his arm.

I pick up the knife,
grab Julio,
and pull him away.

Guerrero's growl rumbles from his throat
like the noise of a bulldozer waking up.
He shakes the man's arm,
making it bleed
worse than the scrape
on Julio's neck
the man made with his knife.

I clench my fists and watch,
not caring how much Guerrero
hurts that man,
because I want him to hurt too.

I hate him,
more than I knew I could hate anyone . . .
for hurting my brother.

So while Guerrero has him pinned,
I kick the man hard.
He bends, moaning,
and grabs his stomach
where I kicked.

Julio and I race away.

Guerrero lets go
and follows us,

leaving the man
behind us, cursing and rolling
in the dirt.

He screams,
"I'll send Immigration
after you!"

I hope he does call Immigration
so they can lock him away
for attempting to transport
immigrants over the border.

Border Patrols

Up ahead, a woman cries out
as she and the man she's with
are pulled into a jeep
by border patrols.

I grab Julio's hand
and move into a stream
as they head our way.

"Duck under," I whisper.
We hold our breaths
and slide behind a bush
and under the water.

I keep my eyes open
and see a jeep move slowly
on the road near us.
It stops at Guerrero,
sitting by the roadside.

A man gets out and scans the area.
He pats Guerrero's head, then says,
"Nothing here," as he steps up into the jeep.

I blow out the air I was holding.
"Come, Guerrero," I say.
"We better head this way."
I pull Julio across the water
and up a hill into the woods
where we wait for night.

There are too many
checkpoints
to travel by day.

Getting Closer

The town we walk through
has some cars with
Texas license plates.

I know we're closer,
and my spirits rise
even though I hand Julio
our last banana.

Nuevo Laredo

Pavement crunches
under the tires of the border patrol
cars as they drive off.

I lead Julio to the river.

It's swollen
from the recent rain
that splashed the park benches
where we slept earlier.

I step into the water
to cool my feet and splash
it over my face to wash.
The current swirls around my legs,
and I watch as a stick floats by.

It spins and dips
before it quickly disappears
under the swells.

"It's too rough to go today," I say,
wondering if it's always this rough.
I look across the river to the banks
of Texas.

We're so close,
but how can Julio cross
this?

How can I?

Mami needs to send
a miracle.

Miracles

I turn to Guerrero.
"Come."
But he doesn't.
He's busy digging
in the sand.
"Guerrero."

He doesn't look up.
He just digs
until I can see
something is there.

A life jacket.

Left by someone who knows
about freedom.

Stories

As a small child,
I heard the stories of
life jackets buried
along the shores
of the Rio Grande.
But I thought they were just
tales,
made up to give
people false hope.

This life jacket
IS REAL,
and so is my
HOPE.

Hope

Julio and I dig
along the banks
for the rest of the night,
hiding every time
we hear the crunching
on the road above,
until we find
another life jacket.

When dawn comes,
we hide the life jackets
and go back to the park
to sleep.

Because tonight
we will go into the river
and swim for our freedom.

Night Crossing

The river is no longer
swollen.
We have to cross.
Now.

We pull our life jackets
from behind the bush
where we hid them
and slip them on.

I tie our pack to my waist
so it can't interfere
with my swimming.

I whisper to Julio,
"I'll hold you,
but when I can't touch the bottom anymore,
we're both going to have to kick hard
and swim like we practiced
in the pool."

"Yes," Julio says.
"Just like the pool.
You'll hold onto me tight?"

"I'll hold on tight," I say.

"Don't let go?"

"I won't ever let you go.
You're my brother,"
I say, as we slip into the
Rio Grande.

"I love you," Julio says.

"I love you."

Giving Up

The current is quick.
It tugs at my feet.
They slide.
I swallow a big gulp
of water and I go under.
Julio slips from my grasp.

I come up, choking
and reaching for him,
but he floats
away
with the current.

"Julio!" I scream.
My voice gets lost
in the crashing of the water
surrounding me.

Julio bobs down the river
and disappears under the water
like the stick
I threw in yesterday.

I race after him,
swimming as hard as I can,
kicking as hard and as fast
as I can
to catch up
to Julio,
but he's going too fast,
and I can't reach him.

I keep kicking
and thrashing with my arms,
but the current pulls me
under the water
until I can't kick
anymore.

Drowning Memories

Beneath the water,
Mami and Papi
and a baby, Julio,
are all in our house
back in the mountains of Guatemala.

Beneath the water,
Papi is playing his marimba,
and we're dancing
and spinning
and smiling.

Beneath the water,
Papi walks
down the mountainside,
away from our village
and us.
And I run down the mountainside
to catch up to him
and beg him not to leave us.
But he just picks me up,
kisses my head,
and says, "I'll come back for you."

Beneath the water,
the soldiers come
and Mami's face clouds over
when we have to leave
the only home
we know.

Beneath the water,
Mami's eyes tear up
when she says we have to live
in the dump.

Beneath the water,
there are hills of garbage
and my friends
and our old couch
and my marbles.

Beneath the water,
Julio dances
in his uniform,
Mami drowns in garbage,
and I play my marimba
for her.

Beneath the water,
Manuel takes us to his farm
and asks us
to stay.
And I pull Julio
away.

Beneath the water
is Pedro's Plaza
and jars of tissues,
and I want one now
to help me forget
everything
I'm seeing.

Beneath the water,
La Libertad plays for me,
and that man attacks Julio.

Beneath the water,
my brother
floats down the river,
and I hate myself for
letting go.

But then,
beneath the water,
I see lights
hovering above me,
and in them
I see Mami.

And Papi yells,
"Come! This way! Come!"

And it's a sign
to go on.
So I kick hard
until my head is
above the water
and I can breathe.

The current pushes me
against a concrete square
in the middle of the river.

I hear footsteps overhead,
and someone yells,
"Did you check over here?"

"It came from over here,"
another person says.

I see lights shining
on the bridge above me.

Immigration.

"There's no one here,"
the man says.
The vehicles pull away,
but I stay
pressed against the concrete square,
unable to move.
Not wanting to move.

It wasn't Papi calling me.
It was the
immigration officers
I heard.

My heart sinks in the river
with Julio.

Lost

I want the current
to wash me away,
but it won't.
It brought me here
and took Julio instead.

It's all
my fault
for not leaving him
at the farm with Manuel.

I was selfish to bring him,
and God is punishing
me by taking him
away from me,
and putting me
here
when I just want to be
with Julio.

So I push off
the concrete block
and let the current
take me.

La Libertad

A bark
from the shore
grabs my attention.

I see them
racing,
trying to keep up
as the current drags me
down the river.

JULIO!

I kick my feet
and keep kicking
until I reach the side of the river.
I grab the vines,
clinging to the bank,
but they snap
and I go under the water
again.

I reach for more vines
and pull myself closer.

Brambles and thorns
rip at my hands,
but I hold tight
and climb until I'm on
the riverbank of
Texas.

I wrap Julio
tight in my arms.
Guerrero jumps on us
and licks my face.

"Texas, Julio.
We're in Texas.
We are free!"
Somos libres

Texas

We sleep in an old barn,
wet, cold, hungry,
and
FREE.

The Texas Sun

When the sun shows its face,
we spread Julio's schoolbooks
out in the sun to dry.

From inside one,
Papi's address
flutters out.

We're lucky
it's still readable.

Miriam

"You best not lie out in the open
if you don't want to get caught,"
a woman says from beside us.

At the sound of her Spanish words,
I jump to my feet
and look at her.

She's smiling
as she gathers Julio's
dried but wrinkled schoolbooks.

"Yours?" she asks me.

"No, his."

She nods and hands them back to us.

"Thank-you," I say
as I put them into my bag.

"Do you belong somewhere?" she asks.

I'm not sure
what she means,
so I just look at the ground
and don't answer.

"Where did you come from?" she asks.

I still don't answer,
but I look at her.

She doesn't look like Immigration.
She's wearing a flowery dress.
But I don't answer
just in case this is how
immigration officers catch people
in the United States.

"I'm not from Immigration,
if that's what you're thinking," she says.
"My name is Miriam.
Are you hungry?"

"Do you poison
illegals here?" Julio asks.

I gasp.

But Miriam laughs.
"So, you are illegals,
and I am still not with Immigration.
Do you need somewhere to stay?
I know of a family."

"We're going to my papi," I say.

"He's here?"

I give her the address.

"It's not far.
I'll phone him to see
if he's still there."

A Phone Call

After two rings,
my papi says,
"Hello."

My eyes tear up,
and I can't find the words
to speak to him.

So I hand the phone to Miriam,
and she talks
for me.

Highways

So many car engines
buzzing in my ears,
intersections colliding
with the main highway,
driving beneath
overpasses and around
cars
        cars
            cars
                    on a Texas highway,
                        going toward Papi.

Papi

Tears stream down
his face
when he sees us.

He runs to us,
arms spread wide,
to whisk us up.

"Libertad?" He places his hands
on my face.
"*Mi Libertad*, that can't be you.
You're so grown."

"It is me,
and Julio too."

"When I went back
and couldn't find you,
I thought I'd lost you
forever."
His strong arms
grasp us close.

"I will never let you go again,
my children."
mis hijos
"Never
again."

Marbles

Deep in my bag,
safe in my old shirt pocket,
I find a shiny marble
I took from the dump
so long ago.

Like that marble,
I've pulled myself
from the dump
and I'm safe,
deep in the pocket
of the United States
with Julio and
mi papi.

Just like Mami wanted.

FREE
from the garbage
FOREVER.

Author's Note

Although this story is fiction, *Libertad* is based on the journey of a real boy named Mariano, combined with other children's actual experiences.

Each year, over 80,000 unaccompanied migrant children attempt to enter the United States. The average age of these children is sixteen, but there are some as young as six or seven – some younger if sent by coyotes. Only a few of these children remain in the US. The rest are deported, usually within two days.

The children who come by way of smugglers, or coyotes, often don't make it into the US or even to the border. Some die as they hide beneath car seats or in small containers, or are left locked in the backs of transport trucks under the hot sun. The largest countries of origin include Honduras, El Salvador, Guatemala, and Mexico.

During my research of the Guatemala City garbage dump, I learned that approximately 10,000 people reside in shacks on the rim of the dump. These shacks are made with whatever can be salvaged from the garbage – tin, cardboard, and broken furniture. Some of these shacks have power, others don't. There are about 100 people who live in large cardboard homes inside the boundaries of the dump. All of the inhabitants make their living recycling garbage, often specializing in looking for specific items like glass, plastic, cans, or cardboard. Children as well as adults work inside the dump.

Because public school in Guatemala costs money, children living in the dump don't often get a chance to attend. Some children are able to attend school because of an organization called Safe Passage.

Safe Passage brings children out of the dump and pays for their tuition, uniforms, and school supplies, allowing them to go to public school for half a day. For the other half of the day, these children attend Safe Passage, where they get a hot meal (most likely their only hot meal of the day) and help with their homework. They also learn skills which will allow them to leave the dump and work elsewhere. Through Safe Passage, children are also able to learn music, play sports, and sometimes go for weekend camping trips. If a child attends school regularly, at the end of each month that child will earn a bag of food to take home to the family. The food provides an incentive for parents to allow their children to stop working and attend school.

Acknowledgments

Thanks to my ducky pals: Kristy Dempsey, Tanya Seale, Katy Duffield, Shelly Becker, Cassandra Whetstone, and Anne Marie Pace, who went through revision after revision of this novel with me. Thanks for being honest when something didn't work.

Thanks to my family: my husband, Claude, and daughters, Jessica and Chantale, for being there during the hours I was overwhelmed by sadness while researching this novel.

Thanks to my agent Leona Trainer, my editor Ann Featherstone, and my publisher Gail Winskill for having faith in this novel.

Thanks to the people who helped me with the Spanish translation: Marta Vartas, Cass, Meg, and Sasha.

And special thanks to Rachel Meyn and the people who work at Safe Passage for reading through *Libertad* for accuracy, as well as to Laura Gardner, MSW, and the other people who work at Bridging Refugee Youth & Children's Services (BRYCS).

DATE DUE
